Meatball

This book is dedicated to
all the children and teachers—
wherever they may be—
from Little Star of Broome
Day Care Center
and
to my dearest life-long friends,
Linda Lowenstein Spielman
and Sally Smith Weiss
pmh

MEATBALL
Text copyright © 1991 by Phyllis Hoffman
Illustrations copyright © 1991 by Emily Arnold McCully
Printed in the U.S.A. All rights reserved.
1 2 3 4 5 6 7 8 9 10
First Edition

Hoffman, Phyllis.
    Meatball / by Phyllis Hoffman ; pictures by Emily Arnold McCully.
       p.   cm.
    "A Charlotte Zolotow book."
    Summary: A little girl describes a typical day at her day care
center.
    ISBN 0-06-022563-7. — ISBN 0-06-022564-5 (lib. bdg.)
    [1. Day care centers—Fiction.   2. Friendship—Fiction.]
I. McCully, Emily Arnold, ill.   II. Title.
PZ7.H6757Me   1991   89-49425
[E]—dc20   CIP
                                                                          AC

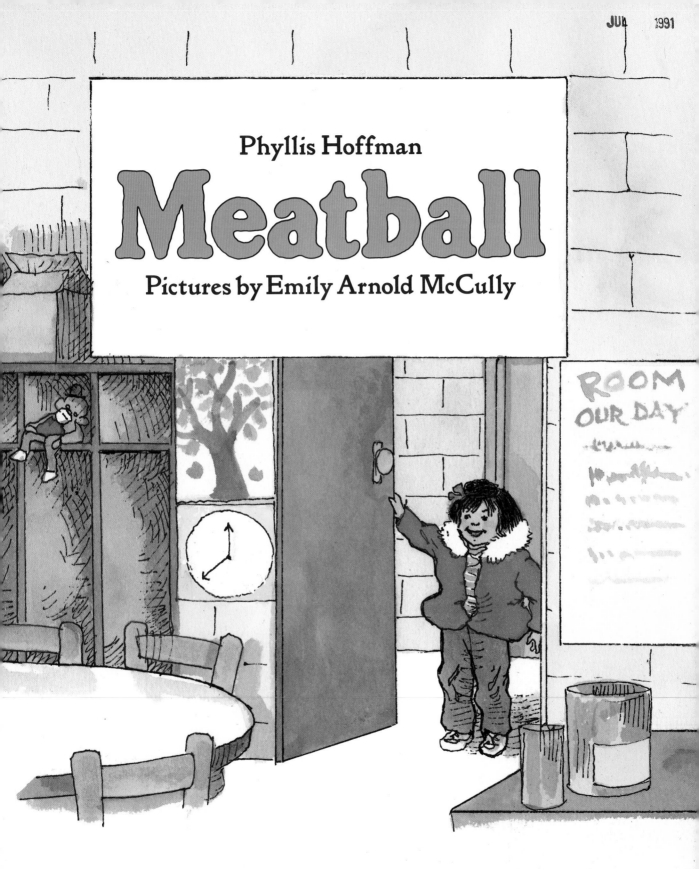

Phyllis Hoffman

Meatball

Pictures by Emily Arnold McCully

A Charlotte Zolotow Book

An Imprint of HarperCollins*Publishers*

My teacher Julia has curly black hair and round wire glasses.
Every day she wears big earrings, a baggy blouse, and
dungarees. In the morning I'm the first one in school.
"Hiya, Meatball!" she says, and gives me a hug. My real
name is Marilyn, but she calls me Meatball because she says
I'm round and yummy.

My mother takes my coat off and hangs it in my cubby for me. Then she rushes off to her school. She is always late. I wave till she's out the front door. I love my mother. I love Julia. And I love Lu.

Lu is my best friend. She is so little. Every day she gets a
ride on her mom's back all the way to the center. When her
mother reaches our room, she throws Lu high in the air, like
a football. Then she gives her lots of kisses and runs out.
Her mother rushes, too! She works in a factory.

When Lu first came to school, she did not speak one word of English. She cried all morning long for a whole month. She wouldn't do any puzzles or drink her milk, or go outside, or play with me. But one day I put my firefighter's hat on her head. It fell over her eyes. Everybody laughed. Lu too. Now we do everything together.

Since Lu and I come early, we get to play together with no one else around. Sometimes we just sit next to each other in our cubbies, with our dolls. Mine is Jessica. Hers is Rita.

Lu's whole name is Soo Fung Lu, but everyone just calls her Lu.

Lu and I like to hold the guinea pigs and feed them while Julia cleans their cage. They are soft and furry, with long front teeth and sharp toenails. We have to put them on pillows to pet them.

Soon everybody starts coming in.
All the children in Room One are
three and four years old. Tony
clings to his mother and screams
when she tries to leave. He cries a
lot, even though he's four.

We take out games until it's
Circle Time. Then Julia holds up
a name card for each child in the
class. I can read. "L" is Lu's
name.

Then we look at our felt board.
Julia points to words as she reads
to us: "Today is Friday. The
weather is _____."
We all say words for the weather.
Hot. Sweaty. Freezing. When it's
raining, you get to put boots on
the boy and girl. Umbrellas, too.

Then we have Sharing. We tell
about new things at home or the
rules at school. We hear a story,
too, and sing songs like "Mary
wore a red dress." When Julia
sings your name, you have to say
what you are wearing, like pink
pants or polka dots. Tony always
says things like "A dumb shirt
with pockets on it!"

RULES FOR SCHOOL

Don't go out of the room.
Don't get off the cot at Rest.
Don't kick cots.
Don't throw blocks.
Don't throw shoes.

During Circle Time, my other
teacher, Mrs. Wang, comes in.
She sets the tables for Snack.

At Snack, not everybody can sit next to a teacher. I sit with Lu. We get peanut-butter sandwiches. Lu licks off the jelly, pulls off the crust, and rolls the bread into a ball before she eats it. Julia says, "That's YUK!"

No one in our class will drink the pulpy orange juice. We love it when we have apple juice. You can make it bubble if you gurgle in it. We clink our glasses together and yell, "Salud!" and drink up.

Then it's Work Time. At Work
you get to choose what to do:
blocks, water table, dress-up
corner, art, or cooking. The water
table is wonderful. You can pour
and pour for hours. Sometimes
we wash our dolls. Once Lu
soaped up her own head and
marched around saying,
"Shampoo! Shampoo!" But Julia
didn't think it was funny.

One time Lu and I played with Robin in the dress-up corner. I was the doctor because the baby was sick, and I got the stethoscope and the shiny black pocketbook. "That's the mother's purse," Robin said. She took it and wouldn't give it back. "I'm not your friend," I cried. "I'm not your friend," yelled Lu. "We're not playing anymore!" We ran to the block corner and left Robin by herself.

At the end of Work you have to clean up. It's my job to
wash the paintbrushes. I love the sink in the bathroom. I
can reach the faucet. If you hold your finger right under it,
the water squirts all over the place.

After everything is put away, we get ready for Outdoors. Lu's big sister Lily is in Room Five. They're in the yard when we are. "There's Lily!" Lu screams. Lily picks up Lu and swings her like an airplane. She won't do me.

Lu doesn't like to play with me outside. She always goes with Lily's class to jump rope. Lu is the only three-year-old who can do Double Dutch! "Look at Lu," Julia screams. "That's my little girl!"

Outdoor time lasts forever,
especially when it's cold.

After a long time, we line up
against the wall and, one by one,
go in to wash up for Lunch.

Two children get to help Mrs. Wang set the lunch tables. Everyone in our class has a job. Pouring the milk is the best one.

I love Lunch. Lu has to sit right next to Mrs. Wang, because she makes Lu eat. If you don't taste a tiny bit of broccoli, you don't get dessert.

When you drink your milk really fast, everybody claps and counts for you: One, two, three, four, five, six, seven, eight, nine, ten! Uno, dos, tres, cuatro, cinco, seis, siete, ocho, nueve, diez! Yah, ee, som, say, um, lō, tsut, ba, gow, sup!

Then Julia hands out the cots. I can carry mine over my head. Mrs. Wang comes around and says, "Shuusshh!" to everybody and tucks you in.

Every day Tony sits on the edge of his cot and cries, "When is my mother coming?" But if I whisper one word to Lu, Julia yells, "There is *NO TALKING* during rest!" Mrs. Wang never yells.

If I'm up a long time, Julia sits next to me. "You're my Meatball," she whispers, and smooths my bangs. Then I turn over and fall asleep.

Once I wet my bed and woke up. Julia said it was okay. She took me to the bathroom and changed my pants, with the door closed. After we washed up, she let me sit on her lap and look at books until it was Milk-and-Cookies Time.

At three o'clock, some children start to go home. Lu's grandpa comes for her and Lily. After Julia leaves, the rest of us do something special with Mrs. Wang. Like making macaroni necklaces.

Tony stands at the window to see how dark it's getting. "My mother's not coming!" he says over and over. He is the last one in the class to be picked up before me. "Your mother is coming at four o'clock," I tell him. "Right, Mrs. Wang?"

"Right," she says, "every day at four."

When his mother walks in, Tony smiles like a light bulb.
Then he leaves, grinning.

On Fridays, my father picks me up. He looks at all my paintings for the week. "A regular Picasso!" he says, rolling them under his arm. He checks my cubby and carries everything for me, except my backpack. Baby Jessica's in there.

When I'm all zipped, he starts talking to Mrs. Wang about what Mom is studying in school. "In fifty more years, I'm going to college, too," I tell Mrs. Wang. "Fifteen," Dad says. I meant fifteen.

I'm so happy when we leave school, because on Friday my father and I always have pizza for supper. And after my bath, I get to stay up and watch TV until nine o'clock when...

my mother comes home.